Acting Edition

The Mamalogues

by Lisa B. Thompson

||SAMUEL FRENCH||

FOR PRODUCTION INQUIRIES

UNITED STATES AND CANADA
info@concordtheatricals.com
1-866-979-0447

UNITED KINGDOM AND EUROPE
licensing@concordtheatricals.co.uk
020-7054-7290

Each title is subject to availability from Concord Theatricals Corp.,
depending upon country of performance. Please be aware that *THE
MAMALOGUES* may not be licensed by Concord Theatricals Corp. in
your territory. Professional and amateur producers should contact the
nearest Concord Theatricals Corp. office or licensing partner to verify
availability.

MUSIC AND THIRD-PARTY MATERIALS USE NOTE

IMPORTANT BILLING AND CREDIT REQUIREMENTS

THE MAMALOGUES received its world premiere co-produced by Color of Arc Productions (Christine Hoang, Artistic Director) and the Vortex Repertory (Bonnie Cullum, Artistic Director) in Austin, Texas, opening on August 23, 2019. The production was directed by Rudy Ramirez. The set design was by Megan Kemp, lighting design by Patrick Anthony, sound design by Johann Mahler, dramaturgy by Virginia Grise, and the stage manager was Cortney DeAngelo. The cast was as follows:

LAUREN HOLMES.....................................Yvonne Oaks

BEVERLY FRANKLIN ....Valoneecia Tolbert

TASHA SIMMONS .... Melody Fullylove

CHARACTERS

LAUREN HOLMES – A forty-eight-year-old African American mother. College professor. Queer. She has a ponytail and is dressed in a classic white shirt, pants, and pricey loafers.

BEVERLY FRANKLIN – A thirty-seven-year-old African American mother. Salon owner. Straight. She has long hair and is wearing a stylish blouse, skirt, and heels.

TASHA SIMMONS – A fifty-one-year-old African American mother. Pediatrician. Straight. She has natural hair (afro, braids, or locks) and is wearing a colorful dress, and comfortable shoes.

SETTING

A cozy bed and breakfast or inn in a suburban town within a major metropolitan area. There's a buffet table laden with coffee, tea, sparkling water, and assorted finger foods and desserts.

TIME

Now.

AUTHOR'S NOTES

Although *The Mamalogues* centers the lives of middle-class Black women, this play is a love letter to all Black single mothers. It is also a story about family, sisterhood, and community among this frequently disparaged group. As the characters convey the disappointments, absurdity and joys of Black single motherhood, never allow the show to devolve into stereotype. The feel of the show should be intense yet playful as it presents each character's fertile imagination and vivid memories. Whenever possible invite the audience to engage as if they are attending the retreat too. The rendering of each vignette should bounce between realism and the hyperreal as the women quickly morph into a myriad of other characters: family members, neighbors, school administrators, and the random strangers that occupy their world. The set should have places to store props for the actors to utilize as they assume different characters.

ACKNOWLEDGEMENTS

Much like a baby, *The Mamalogues* has had a lengthy gestation period. It was initially developed during residencies at Harvard University's W. E. B. DuBois Institute for African American Research, Millay, Hedgebrook, and the Humanities Institute at the University of Texas at Austin. I'm especially grateful to Henry Louis Gates, Jr., Vera Grant, E. Patrick Johnson, Ralina Joseph, Marcyliena Morgan and Cherise Smith for inviting me to share early versions of the play. In 2011 the Hip Hop Archive at Harvard University's W.E.B. DuBois Institute for African and African American Research hosted a pivotal workshop and reading of *The Mamalogues* directed by Colman Domingo and featuring Donnetta Lavinia Grays, Rosslyn Ruff, and Sharon Washington. In 2017 Shirley Jo Finney directed Cymone Love, Carla Nickerson, and Nadine Mozon in a workshop and reading of *The Mamalogues* at the University of Texas at Austin as part of the John L. Warfield Center for African and African American Studies' *Performing Blackness Series*. I also performed solo readings of the work-in-progress at the opening conference of the Center for Communication, Difference and Equity at the University of Washington 2014, and the Black Arts Initiative Speaker Series at Northwestern University 2017.

I'm forever indebted to Christine Hoang, Artistic Director of Color Arc Productions. As lead producer, Christine worked with Bonnie Cullum, the Artistic Director of the Vortex, to bring the show to stage in Austin, Texas. Finally, I'm deeply grateful to family, friends, and colleagues for their support of this project, including: Angela Ards, Sandra Austin, Nyesha Brown, Thais Bass-Moore, Mary Pat Brady, Florinda Bryant, David Campt, Faedra Chatard Carpenter, Adrienne Childs, Nicole Fleetwood, Raymond and Sandra Fontenot, Kevin Foster, Virginia Grise, Deidre Hill-Butler, Christina Knight, Stephanie Lang, Femi Makinde, Tracy Manier, Dwight A. McBride, Marcus McQuirter, Joan Morgan, Sophie Oldfield, Diana Paulin, Rudy Ramirez, Sonnet Retman, Rita Rothman, Valerie Smith, Maury Sullivan, Guy Thompson, Jeffrey Thompson, Robert Thompson, Shirley Thompson, Debra Veley, Omar Wasow, and Isaiah Wooden.

In memory of my grandmother, Bernadine Novella Holmes

and

for my son,

always.

Prologue
Club Women

(Lights up as **TASHA** *enters from the house and mingles with the audience.* **TASHA** *is shortly joined by* **LAUREN** *with whom she reluctantly shares the hosting duties. They have history. Both women casually greet and chat with audience members and engage with them as if they are also attending the retreat.* **TASHA** *and* **LAUREN** *eventually find seats.)*

(While **LAUREN** *speaks* **TASHA** *continues to quietly acknowledge women in the audience, especially any late arrivals.)*

LAUREN. *(Standing.)* Good afternoon! Good afternoon, ladies! I want to welcome you all to this year's BBSM retreat.

> *(***BEVERLY*** *enters and finds a seat.* **TASHA** *waves to her enthusiastically.)*

Please enjoy the spread from Whole Foods. Before you ask, of course there are vegan and gluten-free options for our more discriminating eaters.

TASHA. *(Sitting on the sofa.)* And a slab of ribs for the rest of us!

LAUREN. *(Ignoring* **TASHA.**) I'm thrilled to see so many new faces! It's good to see all of you!

TASHA. Yes, look at all this beautiful blackness!

LAUREN. For some of you this is your first time with us, I want to make sure everyone understands that BBSM stands for Bourgie Black Single Mothers—

TASHA. Not Bad Bitches Starting Mess – unfortunately that name was voted down last year.

    (TASHA sucks her teeth.)

LAUREN. And we don't want to see that posted online ever again, not even in jest!

    (TASHA rolls her eyes.)

This group was established five years ago to provide a place just for us single Black mothers—

TASHA. —of a certain age... *(Winks.)* and a certain income.

LAUREN. At Bourgie Black Single Mothers we come together to share parenting tips, recipes—

TASHA. —complaints about the dating scene in this tired ass town, and good down-home gossip.

LAUREN. Tasha, please. Must you?

TASHA. I must. Are you saying that we can't rant about late child support? Or talk smack about parents who send their kids to school with their hair all wild?

LAUREN. That's not quite right, Tasha. I just think we must foster a positive environment where we celebrate our triumphs instead of always complaining about our challenges.

TASHA. *(To audience)* Well you can call me anytime so we can holler about *all* the drama. Girl, I got you! —

LAUREN. Moving along! *(Gathering herself.)* Since we have so many newcomers let's take a moment to introduce ourselves. Tell us your name, what you do for a living, and anything you want us to know about your children. *(Awkward silence.)* OK. I'll start! My name is Lauren and I'm the current president of BBSM. I'm originally

from San Francisco, I'm an English professor and I
have a son named Alexander. *(Notices* **TASHA** *chatting
with an audience member.)* Since you're in a talkative
mood today, why don't you go next, Tasha?

TASHA. No problem, Ms. Lauren! *(To audience.)* Hi ya'll!
I'm Tasha. I was born and raised in Detroit. I'm the
founder and former President of this little group. Now
I'm the unofficial social secretary. I bring the PARTAY!
I'm a pediatrician. My patients call me Dr. T. Yes, I'm
the one who gives your kids all those shots they hate.
I have a son, and twin daughters. I call them my little
jazz trio but they're more like a rock band. Chile, those
kids get on my—

LAUREN. Thank you, Tasha! Why don't we hear from
some of our other members? *(Approaches a few women
in the audience. Ad libs with them including asking
their name, occupation, how many children they have
etc. After chatting with one or two audience members
she points to* **BEVERLY.***)* Let's hear from you.

BEVERLY. *(*BEVERLY *looks around and slowly stands.)* I'm
new to the group. My name is Beverly. I own a small
business in town—

TASHA. Hey Bev! Tell them about your beauty shop so you
can drum up some more clients!

BEVERLY. It's actually a salon & spa. We provide nail care,
facials, hair care and—

TASHA. Sis, can do some hair too! Color! Weave! Cut!
Even box braids. Tell 'em where it's at, chile.

BEVERLY. Thank you, Tasha. My shop is nearby. It's called
Sweet Cuts. I'm from Houston. H-town, what's good?
I have a daughter named Chelsea. She's six – going on
sixteen!

TASHA. Girl! I know what you mean. These kids do the
most!

LAUREN. Welcome, Beverly, and all—

TASHA. *(To* BEVERLY.*)* Anything else you want to add? Like how you heard about the group?

BEVERLY. Sure! Tasha invited me. She's my daughter's pediatrician.

TASHA. That's right! Give me my props. I'm building community up in here.

LAUREN. *(Trying to regain control.)* Yes! Yes, <u>we</u> are. Thank you, for your contribution, Tasha. *(To the room.)* Welcome to all of our new members. I'm so glad that you're here! Ladies, the theme for today is sharing. Today's retreat gives us a chance for our members to get to know each other better. In my classes I use ice-breakers to facilitate conversation. *(*TASHA *rolls her eyes.)* I placed an assortment of questions in this little basket—

TASHA. That's adorable!

BEVERLY. It is!

LAUREN. *(Showing off a gorgeous rattan basket.)* Thanks! Home Goods!

TASHA. You know that store gets all of my check. All those knick knacks—

BEVERLY. They have nice bedding too.

TASHA. Girl! I can spend hours up in—

LAUREN. We should get back to... *(Motions to the basket.)*

TASHA. Pardon me! Go ahead, Madame President.

LAUREN. I want to remind everyone that the theme for today is sharing. *(To the audience.)* Valerie, stop rolling your eyes!

TASHA. You all game? *(*LAUREN *looks at the audience for approval while* BEVERLY *looks a bit uncomfortable.)*

Scene One
Birth Pains

LAUREN. *(Retrieving a slip from the basket.)* Aw! Here's a good one to start with. Tell us your birth story!

ALL. *(**LAUREN**, **BEVERLY**, and **TASHA** become a chorus of pregnant women engaged in a highly dramatic, loud, rhythmic Lamaze style breathing. Very exaggerated.)* Ha ha ha ha

Ho ho ho ho

Hee hee hee hee

> *(Pause.)*

Ha ha ha ha

Ho ho ho ho

Hee hee hee hee

LAUREN. There is nothing more humbling than meeting new people draped in a hospital gown and panting desperately every three minutes. We've seen it before, but somehow no movie, TV show (or play) has ever represented that delicate dance. You know the one where a woman tries desperately to maintain her dignity—

BEVERLY. While in a hospital gown.

TASHA. *(As nurse.)* "I'm sorry darling, were you sleeping? I just need to draw some blood."

LAUREN. It was a teaching hospital and my doctor was a star on our local public radio station who spewed advice about women's health.

BEVERLY. *(As male doctor.)* "There is rarely a reason to stop being sexually active. You can have sex during your final months of pregnancy, and well into your senior years."

LAUREN. I guess you know why I selected him as my physician.

TASHA. After your water breaks make a mad dash to the hospital into the capable hands of the medical staff. There's nothing left to worry about.

LAUREN. Besides, you already made it through the Godforsaken amniocentesis otherwise known as the—

ALL. "let it be healthy, let it be healthy, let it be healthy—

LAUREN. ...but if it isn't – that's ok, I'll still love it—

ALL. Thank God it's a healthy baby test."

TASHA. What's left to worry about?

BEVERLY. Right! I took all the classes. I packed my bag. *(Tearfully.)* I am officially ready to become a mother.

LAUREN. After setting up the monitors I realize the technician is looking at me askance. Her forehead is wrinkled, her lips are pushed out. What's the problem? Oh, she read my chart and now knows how old I am.

BEVERLY. My worries are temporarily interrupted by— *(Reacts to another contraction.)*

ALL. Awwww!

Ha ha ha ha

Ho ho ho ho

Hee hee hee hee

(Pause.)

Ha ha ha ha

Ho ho ho ho

Hee hee hee hee

BEVERLY. Pushing a baby out of my body is the hardest thing I've ever had to do. How do I summon the strength? My mind races to images from US history. I see the slave quarters – no even worse, a slave ship—

(**TASHA** *and* **LAUREN** *hum mournfully.*)

I begin to imagine the unthinkable. Giving birth in the hull of a slave ship in 1619. The unimaginable. The unspeakable. I begin to think of mothers in prison today. Right now. Pushing as I push, giving birth to babies while wearing leg shackles. And I push. I think of mother's giving birth to still born babies and I push and push and pray and curse and—

TASHA. *(As doctor.)* Push! We can see the head! It's crowning!

ALL. Push! Push!

LAUREN. *(As partner/friend/family member.)* "Honey, push!"

TASHA. *(As nurse.)* "Push!"

BEVERLY. And... *(Heightened pause.)* nothing. I push for over an hour but the baby won't come out.

LAUREN. *(As baby.)* "Ah, no thanks Mom. I'm good."

BEVERLY. There will be no crowning moment, no ultimate release. Instead? There will be drugs and cutting and like 33% of American women in the 21st century – I received a single slash to my abdomen now hidden in my bikini line. Thanks, doctor! Yes, a C-section.

LAUREN. C is not excellent,

BEVERLY. But it does represent a passing grade.

TASHA. Barely.

LAUREN. Yes, pushing out a baby is the single hardest thing that I have <u>never</u> done.

BEVERLY. The nurse holds her over the drape and we meet.

LAUREN. They clean him up and bring these eyes, this body, this voice over to me. It's our moment.

> *(The lighting becomes ethereal.* **TASHA** *cradles an infant.)*

ALL. Baby cries

LAUREN. And mommy cries

TASHA. Partner/Friend/Nana/Nurse, somebody takes pictures—

BEVERLY. Hey, get my good side!

> *(Dramatic West African music plays.*)*

LAUREN. I finally live up to my ancestral past.

TASHA. *(She holds the baby over her head and up to God in a ceremonial fashion, and, in an overly dramatic West African accent says.)* "Behold! The only thing greater than yourself."

BEVERLY. I fulfill my womanly potential I take my place among my sisters in the struggle and I know.

ALL. I am a mother now.

TASHA. Now what?

BEVERLY. Do what comes naturally?

TASHA. *(As cheery nurse.)* "Welcome to Breastfeeding One-oh-One!"

LAUREN. The second most natural act in the world. I'm pumping milk while channel surfing and I land on a news story about people selling breast milk online.

---

* A license to produce THE MAMALOGUES does not include a performance license for any third-party or copyrighted music. Licensees should create an original composition or use music in the public domain. For further information, please see Music Use Note on page 3.

TASHA. Wait! Is that heifer hawking breast milk ice cream? Sweet Lord!

LAUREN. The modern day wet nurse has arrived. I can't imagine feeding somebody else's baby with my breasts! My tatas! My boobs! My mind also turns to the slave quarters—

TASHA. *(As slave woman.)* "Missus slave owner Ma'am, I just cain't suckle little Sandy Mae, and Overseer Jr. too. Besides, I think I have the mastitis. You know. That titty disease?"

LAUREN. What is more unnatural than giving your breast to a complete stranger to suck? I can only imagine an infant tasting breast milk for the first time—

BEVERLY. *(As a mature annoyed baby.)* "No! Wait! This is not what was promised in the magazine ad. Besides, this breast is brown... logically this should be chocolate milk and from what I can tell that is not chocolate milk. Wait? Is this soy? Rice dream? Somebody tell me something because the kid in the bassinet over there is actually very excited. Hey, what's that Similac stuff? Can I get a hit of formula? Come on I heard that the first suckle is free. Wait, I may have a coupon in my diaper bag!"

LAUREN. Yes, there is something actually quite unnatural about motherhood.

Scene Two
Forty

LAUREN. Speaking of unnatural. How old were you when you had your first child?

TASHA. I have nothing to hide! My first baby popped out when I was a thirty three.

BEVERLY. I was thirty one. How about you?

LAUREN. I gave birth to my son at the ripe old age of forty.

TASHA. Yeah, she's a bad chick! The big four–oh!

LAUREN. *(To the audience.)* Anyone got me beat? I won!

TASHA. Look at us! A bunch of old mamas!

LAUREN. It's nearly a fad now, but remember just ten years ago? The whispers?

BEVERLY. *(As a stranger.)* "Was it an accident?"

TASHA. "At that age?"

BEVERLY. "It's a miracle."

TASHA. *(As a southern grandmother.)* "Was you havin' one of them midnight life crises, sweetie?"

LAUREN. *(As a colleague.)* "How dare she at this age? It's just selfish!"

BEVERLY. Absurd.

TASHA. Dangerous.

LAUREN. People always want to know—

ALL. Why the hell did you wait so long?

BEVERLY. "I mean... WHAT IF IT DOESN'T COME OUT ... You know. *(Whispers – loudly.)* Normal?"

LAUREN. And the doctors!

BEVERLY. *(As a doctor.)* "You must know that as a woman of advanced maternal age you will be involved in a geriatric pregnancy."

TASHA. My profession can be a bit shady!

LAUREN. That made me feel so scared.

BEVERLY. "Did you see her baby registry? Does she actually need all of this stuff? Can't she afford to buy her own stroller?"

LAUREN. Yes, I can! But I deserve this bounty after all my hard work. While that twenty-something-couple got pregnant with a wink and a nod, I – like many other women with tufts of gray – spent many nights on my knees praying, and countless hours in doctor's offices suffering through humiliating procedures just so that I can enjoy the miracle of life.

TASHA. I know that's right! I'll never forget the look of smug satisfaction on the faces of my family members. They never believed I'd slow down my career long enough to procreate.

LAUREN. Giving birth gained me entrance into that exclusive club, the sisterhood of motherhood. Yes, now I am truly an authentic Black woman.

BEVERLY. Don't you know a bona fide Black woman is a mama? You know, big mamas, mammies like the burly sister on the pancake box or the one screaming in *Gone with the Wind*!

TASHA. *(In the style of Butterfly McQueen from Gone with the Wind.)* "Miss Scarlet! Miss Scarlet!" *(As herself.)* Yes! We are the Mammies of the world! The bosom of civilization.

LAUREN. And once you have a child those comments about having a baby are quickly replaced by—

BEVERLY. "So, when are you gonna have another? That poor, poor ONLY child."

LAUREN. And my favorite—

TASHA. "I hope that that baby won't derail your career. After all—"

ALL. You ain't no spring chicken!

LAUREN. But it's not all drama. Sometimes motherhood at forty feels victorious. Miraculous. Yes, I'm also part of the "have-it-all" generation!

BEVERLY. Yay! We made it over the finish line before the race was called on the account of faulty eggs. Look at me! I have it all. Lexus hybrid.

LAUREN. Check!

BEVERLY. House in the 'burbs—

TASHA. Check!

BEVERLY. Child with a cute name—

TASHA & LAUREN. Check!

BEVERLY. Fabulous career that gives the false impression of a flexible schedule—

ALL. Check! Check! Check!

LAUREN. But I'm doing this ALL alone. That's not having it all.

BEVERLY. Shush! Please don't tell those size four domestic goddess super moms that I'm barely holding it together.

TASHA. Deal!

LAUREN. Now, if I cross paths with a woman whose baby hunger is palpable, I hold my child so tight his eyes cross. That I am more blessed then anyone deserves becomes clear with each glance from the eyes of my sisters who pray for children, but whose miracle has yet to happen.

BEVERLY. And may never happen.

TASHA. So what do you tell your kids about being a first-time mom at forty?

LAUREN. That's simple. I will answer without hesitation. I've been waiting for you all my life.

Scene Three
Who's Yo Mama?

BEVERLY. That's really beautiful but...

LAUREN. What is it?

BEVERLY. I have a little confession to make.

TASHA. Girl, did you have a booty call last night?

BEVERLY. No, Dr. Tasha. *(Under her breath.)* I wish!

TASHA. Oh well. Come on, fess up!

BEVERLY. This is going to be hard.

LAUREN. Come on. Let's hear it!

BEVERLY. OK. Sometimes I wish I was not a mother. I wish it was just me. Nobody else to worry about. Nobody else to cook for. Cleanup after. To be responsible for. God, I miss the days of staying in bed all day. Buying airplane tickets for one. Shopping for cute outfit only for me. Am I selfish? Am I too broken to be a mom alone? I wonder if I made a mistake.

LAUREN. I hear you. My life is divided cleanly. There was my life BB – before baby – and my life AB – after baby. I can't believe that these two lives were lived by the same woman. It's an extraordinary experience to go from navel gazing... to a different type of navel gazing.

TASHA. Tell it.

BEVERLY. Do I thank God for a healthy beautiful child? All the time, but...

LAUREN. Your kid is still young. It gets easier, Beverly.

TASHA. Don't lie to her. Chile, it doesn't get any easier. My oldest is seventeen and the twins are fourteen. It does not get easier. Ever. It just gets differently hard.

LAUREN. That's true. No matter how you're feeling – today, Beverly. We've got you. Right? *(Motions to* **TASHA** *and the audience.)*

BEVERLY. OK. Here it goes. I hate Mama. I mean I hate the word "Mama."

TASHA. What? Now you done stepped in it!

BEVERLY. Not one matriarch in my family was ever called, Mama. I can't stand it. For me "Mama" evokes do rags, lactation, and cooking over a very hot stove in very small kitchen that you don't own!

TASHA. Watch it!

BEVERLY. Is that wrong? I just despise the sound of that word "Mama." I guess it's too close to "Mammy." My brothers and I always called our mother "Mommy." Not one of us ever called her "Mama."

LAUREN. As long as we are setting the record straight – to be honest. I never called my mother "Mama" either.

TASHA. You fancy Negroes are too much!

LAUREN. We actually called her "Mother." Plain and simple.

TASHA. That seems so formal. So... white.

LAUREN. I prefer proper. Classic.

TASHA. *(Under her breath.)* You would.

BEVERLY. Well, my grandmother was never called "Big Mama" either.

TASHA. Really? Too ghetto? Too reminiscent of pigs feet and pot liquor?

BEVERLY. Maybe.

TASHA. Well I always liked "Moms." "Yo, how's your Moms?" "Your Moms sure can cook!"

LAUREN. Wait, Tasha, your kids don't call you Moms or Mama.

TASHA. You know you're right. They just call me "Mom." Come to think of it, I've been Black for five decades and I can't think of one Black girlfriend who uses "Mama." Some of my white girlfriends do – I don't know what's going on with that exactly.

BEVERLY. One thing I do know is that I am and will forever be "Mommy." So, if somebody asks—

TASHA. Do you love Mama?

BEVERLY. I guess we all have to confess –

ALL. We don't love Mama at all.

Scene Four
Homework

LAUREN. It may be the word "Mama" for you, but you know what sends me over the edge?

BEVERLY. What?

LAUREN. When people ask—

TASHA. *(As stranger.)* "Do you work outside the home?

LAUREN. *(They all laugh.)* Work? Outside the home? Outside? *(To audience.)* Do we work, ladies? Raise your hand if you work! Not only do we work outside the home—

BEVERLY. We work on the side of the home,

TASHA. On top of the home,

BEVERLY. One hundred feet beneath the home!

TASHA. Damn it! We work – period!

LAUREN. And nobody is impressed, least of all other mothers! Professionals and mothers—

TASHA. Professional mother sounds kinda kinky—

BEVERLY. Well, this kinky woman is exhausted!

LAUREN. We could all use some peace, quiet, a lavender scented bubble bath, a slice of molten chocolate cake, and a glass of 1974 Château Lafite-Rothschild.

TASHA. You ain't never lied.

BEVERLY. But I'd feel guilty.

LAUREN. Right! How dare we feel joy?

TASHA. Be ambitious!

ALL. How dare we dream!

TASHA. After all we are living this life we're supposed to be ashamed of.

LAUREN. Our name is on the tongue of every red-faced politician, and we're the subject of every study about the destruction of the Black family.

BEVERLY. We're also the stars of every ghetto movie!

TASHA. *(As stereotypical "bad Black mother." Hand on hip, neck swivels, and sucks her teeth.)* "Lissen, Terrell! I'm not up here to be played with!"

ALL. You gonna leaarrrrnnnnnnnnnn ta-day!

LAUREN. How did we end up here?

BEVERLY. This was not the plan. He seemed like a great guy. He seemed like the one. He loved me more than anyone had every loved me.

LAUREN. They always do.

BEVERLY. But he did. Really did. I just didn't realize that I didn't love him enough to stay... forever. I needed passion. Romance... What did we get instead? Divorce. But not before I had a daughter. My precious girl. I wanted the whole package. Not weekend visitations and co-parenting. Have I failed somehow? *(The other women nod in agreement.)* What's your story?

TASHA. Well I was happily married. Ron was fine.

LAUREN. He was.

> **(BEVERLY** *appears as Ron. Solid, handsome and full of life.)*

TASHA. He was younger than me, smart as a whip and funny as hell. I had it all! A MD, a M.R., and three big beautiful brown babies. Lawd, were we fertile! Did I mention he was fine?

LAUREN. You did.

TASHA. But he went to work and died at his desk. *(Pause.)*

(The light suddenly goes out on Ron.)

Motherfucker!

BEVERLY. Oh my God. I never knew. I'm so sorry for your loss, Tasha.

TASHA. Thanks, girl. Me too. *(**LAUREN** and **BEVERLY** hug her.)*

LAUREN. My story is a bit different. My girlfriend Dana and I were on our way to having it all too. That's until I realized that her all didn't include kids. So we broke up and I decided to stop waiting for Mrs. Right before starting a family. I joined this sorority all on my own. I embraced single motherhood with a gracious donor.

BEVERLY. Good for you.

LAUREN. Well, I thought I knew what I was getting into. I read all the articles, the books, the studies. I entered into motherhood with my eyes wide open. Or at least I thought. But this life? This life right here is more than I bargained for.

TASHA. It doesn't matter how we got here...

LAUREN. Single.

TASHA. Widowed.

BEVERLY. Divorced.

TASHA. The world sees us the same.

ALL. Single. Black. Mother.

LAUREN. I can't help but think about my grandmother. How did she manage as a woman of great dignity but fewer means? A single mother who cleaned some other woman's house and watched HER children and cooked HER meals.

TASHA. And she did all of that so Betty Friedan could be liberated.

LAUREN. When I was in college she sent care packages to keep me going so that I could have a life so much better than she ever imagined.

TASHA. I think of my grandmother, mother, and aunts toiling through endless days and nights.

BEVERLY. How did they do it and retain, not only their pride and sanity, but a sense of grace?

TASHA. How did they manage all of that in the Jim Crow era, before the second wave of feminism, and the invention of GPS?

LAUREN. How did you navigate those times? Can you send word from the great beyond? Heaven, can you send that angel back to me? I need some help finding my way. *(Beat.)* I really miss my mother.

BEVERLY. I miss my mother too. Like a hunger. It hits hardest on holidays. Every Memorial Day I bake her triple-heart attack butter pound cake to start the summer off right. Her voice is in every line of that recipe.

TASHA. *(As* **BEVERLY**'s *mother.)* "Girl, buy the best butter you can afford. Don't you skimp on the vanilla extract either. And make sure the batter looks just right before you pour it in the pan."

BEVERLY. The smell of that cake baking nearly takes me out.

LAUREN. Yeah, the holidays are hard but I can prepare for those because they come like clockwork. But when I catch a scent on the breeze? The sorrow hits out of nowhere. Bam!

TASHA. Girl! Chanel No. 5 on the crook of her neck. Sunday mornings I always caught a whiff while she hurriedly buttoned my coat so we could make it to service on time. Chanel No. 5 makes me seven years old all over again.

LAUREN. For me it's witch hazel. Every night she wiped her freshly washed face with a cotton ball saturated with it. I've been using all these expensive concoctions for years but the other day I decided to get back to basics. That night I stood at my bathroom sink, poured witch hazel onto a cotton ball and had a visitation. The scent took me all the way back to the first time she wiped it on my pimply teenage face.

BEVERLY. The hardest part is knowing that my child will never know her laughter or know her stare!

> (LAUREN *unleashes the certified "Black Mama I'm not playing with you" stare. They all laugh.*)

My baby girl will never know how it feels to have her grandmother brush her hair and grease her scalp as she hums.

> (BEVERLY *begins to hum a sweet blues tune. Other women feel this, nod and make sounds of deep agreement.*)

The moment when she touches your face and you know all is well with the world.

TASHA. Like a prayer.

ALL. Amen.

Scene Five
Let the Church Say

TASHA. Amen is right. *(To* **LAUREN.***)* Have you found a church yet?

BEVERLY. *(As child.)* "Mom, do we believe in God?"

> *(Sounds of pulsing, joyful gospel music*. They are transported to church on Sunday morning.)*

LAUREN. *(Stumped.)* Well, I guess I better find one soon. One of the most important jobs that you ever do for your child is to help them –

TASHA. *(As a Baptist preacher.)* "Find a way out of no way."

LAUREN. At least that's what my grandmother said.

TASHA. Amen!

BEVERLY. These fast-paced modern times call on us to raise our children with a spiritual core.

TASHA. *(As the preacher.)* "Praise Gawd!"

LAUREN. You need to find a place of worship that speaks to your soul. *(Gospel music plays softly.)* In the Baptist church you can find everything that you need to provide your child with a solid Christian foundation. I'm talking about history, redemption, and salvation.

TASHA. *(As the preacher.)* "Beloved, this morning the choir will deliver the glory of Christ through song."

BEVERLY & LAUREN. *(Chanting.)* Nam Myoho Renge Kyo. Nam Myoho Renge Kyo.

---

* A license to produce THE MAMALOGUES does not include a performance license for any third-party or copyrighted music. Licensees should create an original composition or use music in the public domain. For further information, please see Music Use Note on page iii.

TASHA. *(As the preacher.)* "What is that? Please turn your cell phones off! *(Muttering.)* Ain't nobody trying to hear that noise in a house of worship. These chirren ain't got no sense!"

BEVERLY. Namaste.

TASHA. *(As the preacher.)* "What did you say? Beyoncé?"

LAUREN. I hadn't been to church for years. I practice yoga and meditation. but I knew something was missing. Something that had shaped my young soul.

BEVERLY. *(As Black radio DJ.)* "Welcome to the Gospel Hour on WBLK where we play Mahalia Jackson, Edwin Hawkins, the Clark sisters, and the Reverend Shirley Caesar."

(Classic Gospel music begins to play softly*.)

The sweet sounds of glory. Thank you, Black Jesus!

LAUREN. *(Reveling in the song.)* Those are the sounds of my childhood. I loved being in the choir at Good Sheppard Baptist Church. We sung all the songs I loved as a girl.

TASHA. *(Singing.)*
BLESSED ASSURANCE, JESUS IS MINE.
O WHAT A FORETASTE OF GLORY DIVINE
HEIR OF SALVATION, PURCHASED OF GOD
BORN OF HIS SPIRIT, WASHED IN HIS BLOOD

ALL. *(Singing.)*
THIS IS MY STORY, THIS IS MY SONG
PRAISING MY SAVIOR ALL THE DAY LONG

---

* A license to produce THE MAMALOGUES does not include a performance license for any third-party or copyrighted music. Licensees should create an original composition or use music in the public domain. For further information, please see Music Use Note on page iii.

LAUREN. One Sunday morning the service took a left turn—

TASHA. *(As the preacher.)* "I said that the Lord didn't create Adam and Steve. I believe the names were Adam and much later from his rib, the Lord brought forth his female companion, his helpmate, Eve."

LAUREN. *(As the preacher.)* "Now you got these folks out here fornicating, sodomizing and what not and then asking for the blessed sacrament of MARRIAGE? It's an abomination!

BEVERLY. *(As the preacher.)* "Black women can't find husbands because these so called men are out here marrying each other. You better take that mess somewhere else!"

LAUREN. So I took my child somewhere else praying that I'll find a righteous elixir to guide my spirit. I want a church with the soulful sounds of the Mighty Clouds of Joy—

ALL. *(A church organ punctuates every utterance.)* Amen!

LAUREN. The communal pleasure of call and response—

ALL. Preach!

LAUREN. Church mothers dishing up soul food in the fellowship hall after the service—

ALL. Glory!

LAUREN. As well as a moment or two for quiet contemplation, meditation and maybe some crystals—

TASHA. What? Have you gone lost your cotton pickin' mind!

LAUREN. Yes! You see I just want to make sure that the call my child responds to – that my baby hears is truly righteous, courageous, loving and welcoming.

TASHA. "Black woman! Black woman! You wondering why you're alone? You don't know how to love a man and place him at the head of your household. You've got to SUBMIT! You'll never keep a man if you trying to wear the pants!"

LAUREN. Listen Rev, I like wearing pants sometimes and I love heading my own household.

TASHA. *(As the preacher.)* "Don't follow those pro-choices folks. Out here slaughtering babies! Have them babies Black women, for when we are old and weary they will be the warriors that will protect our community."

LAUREN. Okay Rev, but who will protect us from you? *(Beat.)* No, the search for a house of worship has not been easy.

TASHA. *(As the preacher.)* "Then you got some women are out here having babies on they own like they can be the mother AND the father."

LAUREN. I pray for a church home with soulful gospel music and gay couple support groups, yoga workshops AND fried chicken in the basement. I want a Sunday school were imaginative folk teach our sons and daughters the glory of prayer and faith. A space with a tutorial lab and a meditation room painted purple. Not only do I want my son to appreciate the choir's gospel sway, but I also want him to embrace the silent wisdom of Tibetan monks.

BEVERLY. The hustle these days means moving for career opportunities and leaving behind trusted pillars.

LAUREN. You hope your new life will grant you something almost as good – dare I say better? I don't see that on the horizon.

TASHA. *(As the preacher.)* "Oh Lord, my Lord!"

(Gospel organ begins to build to a crescendo.)*

"Congregation, are you there? Pick up! Pick up! Jesus is on the mainline!"

---

* A license to produce THE MAMALOGUES does not include a performance license for any third-party or copyrighted music. Licensees should create an original composition or use music in the public domain. For further information, please see Music Use Note on page iii.

Scene Six
Traveling Mercies

BEVERLY. Yes, you've got to pick up the phone and call on Jesus—

(Sounds of a busy airport.)

when you're traveling with your kids.

LAUREN. Absolutely! There was traveling before motherhood—

BEVERLY. *(Lays the back of her hand over her forehead dramatically.)* "I'm so busy."

LAUREN. —and there is travel after.

BEVERLY. Damn it! Where did I leave my— *(Frisking her pockets looking for that elusive something.)* child?!

LAUREN. We're easy to spot.

TASHA. There's one now! Moving fast!

LAUREN. Today's career woman arrives at the airport with her expensive carry-on bag while rolling her eyes at the other people in line. Her prime adversaries? A family of four comprised of two parents, a brooding pre-teen and a twisting, screeching toddler.

TASHA. Wait! Stop! Is that child… on a leash? It's not an animal, my God. If you can't leave the house without a bridle then maybe your family shouldn't be traveling.

LAUREN. Traveling while Black and with a child is especially helpful on those "select your own seat" airlines. I love the fear I instill when they see us walking down the aisle.

BEVERLY. "Look! A single Black woman with a baby!"

(They all scream in horror!)

LAUREN. It's not like I was very popular before I had a child, but now the blissfully empty seat besides us seems to be carcinogenic.

TASHA. "NO, that's okay. I'll take that middle seat near the bathroom with that huge wad of bubble gum on the headrest."

LAUREN. Flying since the ripe old age of three months, actually my child is beautifully behaved – on most flights. I can't say the same for my fellow passengers.

BEVERLY. Did you hear about that white man on that Delta flight a few years back who slapped that Black baby because he was crying?

LAUREN. Yes! That crazy fool slapped a Black baby after he called him the N word!

TASHA. Oh hell naw! I wish a muthafucka would try to slap my child! Y'all would have to put money on my books at the jailhouse for real.

LAUREN. You ain't never lied!

TASHA. Girl, I'd be locked up but that bastard would be six feet under!

BEVERLY. What kind of world is this? Now we gotta worry about somebody brutalizing our infants at thirty thousand feet.

TASHA. And we don't even get a meal on the damn flight!

Scene Seven
Terror in the Suburbs

TASHA. Traveling can be hell but you know what's else is scary?

> *(Sounds of young children playing at the park.)*

LAUREN. Pools and parks!

BEVERLY. Agreed!

LAUREN. Here is my unofficial, very unscientific analysis. After visiting pools and playgrounds in Cambridge, Chicago, Austin, San Francisco, Portland, and Seattle, the further west you travel the more likely your little angel will be an OBC. *(To the audience.)* You know what that is!

ALL. Only Black child.

TASHA. Right. Wait, what about Oakland?

LAUREN. Gentrified!

TASHA. Damn!

LAUREN. Here's how it usually goes.

BEVERLY. *(As mother in the park observing* **LAUREN.***)* "Lululemon duds, Birkenstocks, two-carat diamond studs, a stylish backpack—"

TASHA. *(As another mother.)* "And organic snacks. Hmm."

BEVERLY & TASHA. "What's her story?"

BEVERLY. *(To* **LAUREN.***)* "I haven't seen you before. Are you new around here?"

LAUREN. *(To the other mother.)* Yes. *(To audience.)* I've been spotted!

BEVERLY. "Wow! He's quite a swimmer."

LAUREN. Thanks.

BEVERLY. "How old is he?"

LAUREN. Six.

BEVERLY. "Wow! Hey there, big guy! Are you going to be a football player? A basketball player?"

TASHA. *(As child.)* "No, I'm going to be a physicist."

BEVERLY. *(To child.)* "You don't say." *(To mother.)* "Well, good for you!"

LAUREN. That's the stay-at-home Moms. Wait until the nannies at the park get a bead on me. They try to locate my blond, blue-eyed charge, instead they spy my nappy headed darling and reality sets in.

TASHA & BEVERLY. *(As nannies.)* Ohhhhh!

LAUREN. Once the preliminaries are over the playground small talk really begins. It starts out innocent enough.

BEVERLY. *(As a mother in the park.)* "Good news! I heard a new Trader Joe's opened!"

LAUREN. Inevitably you find yourself hemmed up by the slides being queried about the aesthetic aims of Tyler Perry—

BEVERLY. The upcoming rap concert.

> *(TASHA and LAUREN freeze momentarily in an exaggerated "hip hop" pose.)*

LAUREN. The Obama presidency.

TASHA. "I wish he could do four more years! No, eight more!"

LAUREN. Or my hair!

BEVERLY. "Today you have braids. Last week you had an afro. How do you do it?"

LAUREN. *(Beat.)* But, once in a while you fall in love. Gazing across the grassy circle you catch each other's eyes and laugh at the same thing. You pocket your iPhone, she logs off Instagram, and the two of you actually talk.

BEVERLY. Mommy to mommy.

TASHA. Woman to woman.

LAUREN. And if you're lucky it actually becomes cherished chats and stolen moments on soccer fields, across Chuck E. Cheese tables and whispers at the back of the library during story time.

BEVERLY. Friend to friend.

LAUREN. Once in a blue moon. Some wonderful miracle happens and you meet a mommy that gets you. No mommy wars. No competition. It's not fraught. It's not complicated. It's mother love. *(Beat.)*

TASHA. Then it happens.

LAUREN. Something hits the news and she says something that pushes you off the integration tight rope.

BEVERLY. Your comments are carefully honed. Not too bitchy. Not too revealing. You share what you can and you hope she doesn't ask too much.

TASHA. You wonder if your visits on the playground entitle her to stories about your torrent of tears on that election night in 2008. Your nightmares about George Zimmerman. Your belief in reparations.

LAUREN. Are we girlfriends or are these moments simply an extension of her Bryn Mawr Anthropology 101 course? Is this really love, or just infatuation?

ALL. *(In unison.)* I thought you were different.

LAUREN. After the calls stop, and the stolen moments end, we still have to maintain a relationship because of the children. You can't just break up... the friendship. Instead you find a way to make it work even though it doesn't work anymore. You see each other at the birthday parties and you suffer through pre-arranged play dates. It's back to small talk about shopping and the refs at the latest softball match. *(Beat.)* But all that awkwardness evaporates when there is a tussle, cry, scream, or scrape.

(Alarm sounds.)

TASHA. Battle stations everyone!

BEVERLY. Every mom has a moment when she cannot find her little one in the running, screaming, frolicking mass of baby fat and snotty noses. The heart stops! Ice runs through her veins like <u>bad smack</u> (not that I know, but it sounds really cool).

TASHA. *(Hand covers a Secret Service agent style earpiece.)* This is a code red! I cannot get a visual! The threat alert is elevated. I repeat, the threat alert is elevated.

LAUREN. How can your heart stop and race at the same time? It's excruciating agony. It's the longest twenty-three seconds of your entire life.

BEVERLY. You scan the playground like a hawk. Your body swivels back and forth with upmost speed – those yoga and Pilates sessions were not in vain. You climb on a park bench and stand on your tippy toes to gain the best possible vantage point.

TASHA. *(Hand covers ear piece.)* Wait! There he is. I have the target. We have a visual. Fourteen yards due southeast. He's near the swings and sandbox. Stand down. He's all right.

ALL. Thank God!

LAUREN. No crazy ass somebody traipsed off with my little prince. *(They participate in a collective and audible heavy sigh.)*

TASHA. But what if he was missing? I find it hard to imagine a news anchor wringing her hands as she testifies to the purity and innocence of a missing little Black boy.

BEVERLY. *(Nancy Grace imitation.)* We are missing a Negro – I'm sorry – a Black African American child, male. Is that right, Kirsten? Yes, it's a small African of American heritage who was <u>allegedly</u> playing in the park. *(Examines notes.)* Hmm. That's a good neighborhood too. You usually don't find those kind of people, I mean that kind of thing happening there.

LAUREN. When was the last time the authorities released an Amber alert for a missing Black boy? What do they even call it?

TASHA. A Tyrone alert?

LAUREN. A Rasheed response?

BEVERLY. An Antoine alarm?

LAUREN. No, there is no alert for abducted Black boys.

TASHA. But everybody is on the lookout for them – to cause trouble. If a Black boy talks too loud…

BEVERLY. Moves too fast…

LAUREN. Or acts too energetic…

TASHA. There is no timeout or warning. Instead?

ALL. There will be consequences.

BEVERLY. If there is no "school safety officer" to subdue him they will promptly send the child to the principal's office. There he'll receive a suspension, a referral for some ADD meds topped off with a call to a behavioral therapist—

TASHA. Or, worse—

ALL. The police.

TASHA. This completes our tour of the school to prison pipeline. Have a nice day! *(They all wave cheerily.)*

BEVERLY. Yes, we are parenting while Black and living in the age of anxiety.

TASHA. Wait! "The age of anxiety?" Really? That's such a grand self-indulgent phrase. It's spoken like this is some kind of a unique moment in American culture. Black parents were a bit anxious when the Klan was outside the door.

BEVERLY. And we can't forget about the era of school desegregation?

TASHA. What desegregation?

LAUREN. How dare I complain? My child attends the best suburban school within a two-hundred-mile radius. My biggest concern is whether he receives fair treatment at the science fair. *(Beat.)* Nothing to fear here.

TASHA. No Amber Alert. According to news reports nobody is taking innocent little Black boys and girls off America's streets. But they are dying anyway.

BEVERLY. Chicago?

LAUREN. Can we save them?

TASHA. Oakland?

LAUREN. Will we save them?

BEVERLY. New York?

LAUREN. Anyone trying to save them?

ALL. Memphis? Cleveland? Philadelphia? Detroit? Atlanta? New Orleans? St. Louis? Houston? Baltimore? America?

BEVERLY. Do you want to save them? Any of them?

TASHA. Can we get an Amber alert for Tanisha and Tyrone?

LAUREN. Everyone cried for Polly Klaas, Caylee Anthony, Natalee Holloway and Amber Hagerman, but nobody cries for brown babies.

BEVERLY. How could we when missing Black girls never make the news?

ALL. Say her name!

TASHA. And little Black boys? Well, we know their fate.

LAUREN. Our friendships will always have unfilled silences because they don't know what it feels like to be missing and never sought after.

ALL. *(Furiously waving goodbye.)* See you at the park!

Scene Eight
The N word

TASHA. What's the worst moment that you ever experienced as a mother?

BEVERLY. *(As child.)* "Mommy! Mommy! What's a nigger?"

LAUREN. Ah. The four hundred-year-old question. So, how did Mommy answer that one?

BEVERLY. I remember when I first heard it. I was in kindergarten. I was wearing my pink polka dot dress and a white satin bow and a buttercream ivory slip – a slip, remember those? White stockings and squeaky snow-white patent leather shoes. My four ponytails braided and bangs, banging. I mean the do was tight! I was pressed and curled and ready to shine! Okay, I don't really remember all of that. I only recall it with such stunning detail because it was picture day. Yes, I have a photo to commemorate the day somebody first called me—

TASHA & LAUREN. *(As the school bully.)* "Niggggggerrr!"

BEVERLY. The word was spat at me by the girl all the kids called—

ALL. Dirty Mary!

TASHA. *(As Dirty Mary.)* "My Mama said your skin is Black because NIGGERS. Don't. Wash."

BEVERLY. I was completely appalled and especially mortified because SHE said it to me. Mary was a portly, unkempt, blond and ruddy bully. What she lacked in style she made up for in meanness. Mary's family rented that house on the corner with the peeling yellow paint and patch of dirt where the grass should grow. It was rumored that Mary had poor hygiene. I don't know because I never got close enough to her to find out. I was shocked when Mary said—

TASHA. "Your skin is Black because NIGGERS. Don't. Wash."

BEVERLY. Black people don't wash? We don't wash? That's strange because I remember being soaped, soaked and scrubbed until a rash developed. Then I was slathered with lotion.

LAUREN. Jergens!

BEVERLY. And oiled—

LAUREN. With Vaseline.

BEVERLY. Until I slipped effortlessly into my clean undies. I was brushed and combed each morning and night until I sparkled. Excuse me? Do you see what I am wearing? How can *she* disparage me?

TASHA. So what did y'all tell your kids about THAT word?

LAUREN. Not yet. He's too young, besides I don't use it myself.

TASHA. Really?

LAUREN. No, I don't. Do you?

TASHA. Well, there's the N word and the friend word. You know, nigga. You gotta teach them the complex difference between the two. The despicable term and term of endearment. My kids know the difference.

BEVERLY. You can do as you wish, but I couldn't discuss that word with my baby girl. I told her not to worry about it. I don't want to cripple my child with the horrors of American history and the twenty four-hour news cycle littered with Black bodies.

LAUREN. It's just too much.

TASHA. Well, we can't stay silent. Are you going to wait until somebody like Dirty Mary does the honors? It's hard but folks must find ways to talk with their Black, brown, yellow, and especially white children about race.

BEVERLY. Not yet. Not yet.

TASHA. What if a stranger approaches your daughter on the street and wants to give her candy?

BEVERLY. I already told her if that happens that she should run like hell!

TASHA. Did you tell her to run outside if the building catches on fire?

BEVERLY. Of course!

TASHA. What's the difference? No child should face that word without the proper training.

LAUREN. Well, I'm going to give my baby boy the best offense and defense. I'll shower him with all the "you are Black and beautifuls" that his little ears can hold.

TASHA. *(As child.)* "Mommy, what should I say if somebody calls me a nigger?"

BEVERLY. Tell them—

ALL. Your Mama!

Scene Nine
Camp

TASHA. Whew! Somebody better pray for me because summer is coming and I've got three kids at home. Jesus!

BEVERLY. Call on the Lord and He will deliver the answer.

> *(Kitschy infomercial music plays* as* **BEVERLY, TASHA,** *and* **LAUREN** *become hyper sales people.)*

> *(As Camp Race R Us Spokesperson.)* "Tired of sending your brown little jewel to integrate yet another camp? Are you struggling to raise healthy, balanced, smart, happy and nappy American children?"

ALL. Welcome to Camp Race R Us!

TASHA. *(As Camp Race R Us spokesperson.)* "We realize what it takes to raise a Black child in America. You can't allow them to have fun, play videogames, or plop them in front of the television EVER! Daydream? Have you lost your mind?"

BEVERLY. "Maybe! The high school dropout rate for Black boys is at epic proportions and Black girls are punished in school more harshly than any other group. In this world of pre-school entrance exams, helmets, knee-pads, and Latin tutors, you can't allow your Black child to experience the summer slide.

LAUREN. *(As Camp Race R Us spokesperson.)* "But don't you worry! We will help your little brown Brainiac slaughter the SAT and the ACT, but we provide more than academic enrichment. You see I started this

---

* A license to produce THE MAMALOGUES does not include a performance license for any third-party or copyrighted music. Licensees should create an original composition or use music in the public domain. For further information, please see Music Use Note on page iii.

company because strangers kept approaching me at Whole Foods asking for help. How do you do it? Your child seems so smart, well balanced, happy, and so... Black. I mean just the right amount of Black".

TASHA. "Yes, it's essential to teach your Black child how to be Black. This doesn't come naturally you know, especially if you're raising your Black baby in the 'burbs."

LAUREN. "By the time they enter school they must be well versed in the dynamic of racial victimhood. They need to know how to—"

ALL. *(Delivered Wheel of Fortune style.)* Play! The! Race! Card!

TASHA. Not picked for dodge ball?

ALL. Racism!

BEVERLY. Always it during tag?

ALL. Racism!

LAUREN. Nobody will sit with you during lunchtime?

ALL. Racism!

TASHA. No teachers or administrators of color at the school?

ALL. Ra—

(Music stops abruptly.)

BEVERLY. Hey y'all, all of that could actually be racism.

LAUREN. You're right. *(They all nod furiously.)*

(Music resumes.)*

---

* A license to produce THE MAMALOGUES does not include a performance license for any third-party or copyrighted music. Licensees should create an original composition or use music in the public domain. For further information, please see Music Use Note on page 3.

BEVERLY. "When your child grows a bit older and reaches the pre-teen years Camp Race are Us provides a special session for those who lack first-hand experience with persistent racial violence. Our most popular session?"

ALL. Police harassment.

BEVERLY. "At this exclusive session, young boys are given elite training on how to lie face down on the pavement, put their hands behind their necks and say —"

LAUREN. "Yes sir!"

BEVERLY. "—loud enough to be heard even when a peace officer has a knee in his back. Your sons will also learn to NEVER reach for anything in his pocket – EVER. Repeat after me young Black men."

ALL. NEVER reach for anything in your pocket EVER!

BEVERLY. "—because it just may be the last thing you ever do." *(Beat.)* Rest in peace.

ALL. Amadou.

BEVERLY. Rest in peace.

ALL. Trayvon.

BEVERLY. Rest in peace.

ALL. Sean

BEVERLY. Rest in peace.

ALL. Oscar

BEVERLY. Rest in peace.

ALL. Michael, Eric, Freddie, Walter, Philando, Tamir.

(*Pause.*)

BEVERLY. "Don't worry your daughters won't be left out at Camp Race R Us. Your daughter will emerge able to navigate the intersection of racism and sexism and be able to detect whether she's facing discrimination because she's Black or a woman –"

TASHA. "– or both."

> (**LAUREN** *and* **TASHA** *demonstrate each behavior as* **BEVERLY** *describes them.*)

BEVERLY. "If girls opt for the Sandra Bland track, they will learn how to resist the urge to engage in the following behaviors: finger pointing, hand on hip, neck rolling, teeth sucking and eye cutting when encountering a white person working in an official capacity."

TASHA. This is important knowledge.

LAUREN. "Girls will also make quilts adorned with the names of our fallen sisters, daughters, mothers, and grandmothers."

ALL. Rekia Boyd, Korryn Gaines, Charleena Chavon Lyles, Aiyana Jones, Eleanor Bumpers.

TASHA. (**TASHA** *thrusts her fist high and the others join her.*) Rest in power.

BEVERLY. "Wait there's more. At Camp Race Card we can show your little one how to avoid being picked on by their *(Fist pump.)* "I am blacker than you" cousins. *(Super corny.)* Yes, an afternoon session can teach your little one to twist up a joint like Snoop Dog. Wait, a little too real? Don't worry, It's not really weed, only parsley."

TASHA. "As for classroom exercises? There are plenty! Topics include:"

LAUREN. "How to spot a teacher who expects very little from you because of your high melanin count."

BEVERLY. "They will learn how to tell your Mama jokes, cornrow, and make red beans and rice—"

LAUREN. "Yum!"

TASHA. "Finally, they will be taught how to challenge the librarian about the lack of books featuring Black people. Sorry, Negro History Month selections do not count."

LAUREN. "There is no reason for your darling to navigate the changing racial climate on their lonesome. Our devoted culturally competent counselors will answer all of their troubling little questions about what it means to be Black in the #BlackLivesMatter era."

BEVERLY. "Yes, at Camp Race R Us your little BAP – bourgie American prince or Black American princess – will become a militant/athlete/culturally aware thug, and maintain a 4.3 GPA, all while nurturing their artistic side."

LAUREN. "Send your baby to Camp Race R Us this summer!"

TASHA. "Enroll now!"

BEVERLY. "Spots are going fast."

LAUREN. "They are guaranteed to leave ready to play a card—"

ALL. "Any race card!"

(Hip hop beat begins to play.*)

---

* A license to produce THE MAMALOGUES does not include a performance license for any third-party or copyrighted music. Licensees should create an original composition or use music in the public domain. For further information, please see Music Use Note on page iii.

Scene Ten
So Fresh and So Clean

TASHA. Whew! I've been triggered.

BEVERLY. Me too!

TASHA. I'm craving something... sweet. (*TASHA sorts through the food on the table.*)

BEVERLY. (*Slathers brie on a cracker. Holds it up for all to see.*) Yes, but I prefer savory. I can't live without good cheese. That calms my nerves.

LAUREN. Yes, comfort food always takes the edge off. I just don't know what I want.

TASHA. (*Finds a box of chocolates.*) There it is! A big hunk of dark, thick... chocolate. (*Everybody laughs. To* **LAUREN** *mockingly.*) I know what really calms you down, Miss Lauren.

LAUREN. Don't you dare!

TASHA. (*As* **LAUREN**'s *housekeeper.*) "Do you need anything else, Miss Lauren?"

LAUREN. No. That's it, Susie. Thank you so much for everything.

TASHA. "Of course, Miss Lauren.

LAUREN. "I don't know how I'd be able to manage without your help. You save my life every week! I do have one favor to ask. Susie, can you please stop calling me, Miss? Lauren. Just Lauren."

TASHA. "OK, Miss. I mean... Lauren."

LAUREN. How is your son doing in school?

TASHA. "I miss him so much. Everyday. He calls me from the college and he says, Mama! Send me one of your pies. Mama, I can't find any clean clothes. Mama, can you pay my cell phone bill? That boy!"

LAUREN. I can't believe he's already in college. Wow. You must be so proud! Here you go, dear. *(Hands her an envelope.)* Thank you again for everything.

TASHA. "Thank you so much, Miss. *(Notes the additional money.)* You are too kind."

LAUREN. You deserve every bit. Those college textbooks are expensive!

TASHA. "Yes, they are. Thank you again. See you next week... Lauren!"

LAUREN. *(Beat. To her friends.)* She's my rock. A few days after Susie cleans my house it's a total mess. But the minute she leaves, I look around and don't touch a thing. I just sit in my living room and admire her handiwork and breathe. *(Beat.)* Am I less of a woman because I allow another to clean my stove, wipe down my countertops, mop my floor, empty my trash and *(Whispers.)* scour my toilets?

TASHA. Maybe.

LAUREN. It took me decades to discover that my grandmother, my regal grandmother did the same work – day work they called it back then – to keep my mother and her four little brothers fed. She hid it from us. She and my aunts told us they were nurses. Grandma used to tell me stories about the family she worked for. Somehow it never occurred to me that nobody hired nurses with a junior high school education.

BEVERLY. *(As Grandma.)* "Those folks relied on me to keep that big old house from going to the dogs. They needed me to keep em alive! Without women like me this entire country would fall apart!"

LAUREN. I often wonder what Susie really thinks about me.

TASHA. *(As she finishes cleaning materials and packing up hand me downs clothing.)* "She thinks I want her old clothes and used furniture. I work for what I have. I don't beg. I don't ask. I don't need hand me downs! I don't have a husband either. We aren't any different in that regard. A little extra? I deserve every cent and more. She's not as bad as the rest, but sometimes I can smell her guilt as soon as she opens the door. It stinks. I want to tell her: you don't need to feel ashamed. Relax. Sister, I'm proud of the work I do. I wish you were proud of it too. But that's not my job."

Scene Eleven
Much is Expected

BEVERLY. *(To* LAUREN.*)* Can I ask you something?

LAUREN. Sure.

BEVERLY. What's really important to you besides being a mother?

LAUREN. My writing. It keeps me sane and allows me to make order of the world. If I had to say, it would be that.

BEVERLY. *(To* TASHA.*)* And you?

TASHA. My community. Giving back is essential. It feeds my soul. What's that saying? *(Places her hand to her ear to encourage audience participation.)* "To whom much is given..."

ALL. "Much is expected."

TASHA. Yes, that's right! Y'all got some good home training. Now let me ask you something. If I am my ancestors' wildest dreams then why am I still dealing with their worst nightmares? *Some* people are surprised when I tell them that I'm a doctor.

LAUREN. *(As a stranger.)* "Do you practice on people?"

TASHA. No, I practice on dolls until I can work myself up to taking care of humans.

LAUREN. "Oh."

TASHA. But when I tell <u>my</u> people I'm a doctor they respond differently.

BEVERLY. *(As* TASHA*'s patient, Yonnie.)* "Yes, she's a doctor. A good ass doctor too."

TASHA. I've been in private practice for twenty years but I also volunteer on a health mobile where we give general medical attention to those who are in need.

BEVERLY. What's up Dr. Teeeee!

TASHA. She was my favorite on again off again patient.
Let's just call her—

BEVERLY. *(Quite loud, bodacious, ratchet and lovely
patient.)* "Yonnie. But you can call me, Yon! You know,
like you're tired."

TASHA. After a long day of seeing patients, she made me
feel like I was sixteen again and wild. *(To* BEVERLY.*)*
You didn't finish the forms, Yonnie.

BEVERLY. "I ain't trying to do all that, Doc. Come on. You
just ask me shit and I'll tell you shit. Is that cool?"

TASHA. You still working at the Pancake House?

BEVERLY. "Pancake House? Naw, Doc. I stopped working
there months ago. I'm doing online training to be a
dental hygienist. I'm gonna be wearing a little white
coat like you soon!"

TASHA. Yonnie, what is the first day of your last menstrual
period?

BEVERLY. "Damn, can you buy me a drink first before
you're all up in my business?"

TASHA. You know how this goes.

BEVERLY. "A few weeks ago? Maybe."

TASHA. OK. Hmm. Do you have breast tenderness? Are
you experiencing fatigue?

BEVERLY. "Uh huh. I'm tired all the damn time but that
ain't nothing new."

TASHA. So, we should do a test.

BEVERLY. "Fine. *(Beat.)* How much school did you do to
become a doctor? It must have been like, forever."

TASHA. Almost.

BEVERLY. "You happy looking at women's private parts all day?"

TASHA. It's an honor to take care of women and help them take care of themselves.

BEVERLY. "I heard that. Folks gotta call you doctor too so that's dope."

TASHA. *(To* BEVERLY.) You're thirteen weeks pregnant.

BEVERLY. "Really? Lucky thirteen. And that means—"

TASHA. It means you will have another beautiful baby in six months.

BEVERLY. "And?"

TASHA. It's too late to terminate.

BEVERLY. "Terminate?"

TASHA. I can also share information about adoption.

BEVERLY. "Give my baby up? Naw, I'm good, Doc. Keep that information. Tell me where I can find me a job with some health insurance and some maternity leave. I hope it's a baby girl. I've always wanted a girl. I could braid her hair, teach her how to double-dutch and play jacks. What? Don't look at me that way. I've got this. It's all good!"

TASHA. I invited her to my private practice. The staff twisted their lips up some but nobody said anything. She came when she could.

BEVERLY. "I'm doing the best I can! Damn! If I don't show up to work, I don't get no check. I can't feed my children on medical appointments. I'm doing good. I eat, I sleep when I can, I take those huge ass pills."

TASHA. Prenatal vitamins.

BEVERLY. "Whatever. They give me gas."

TASHA. And drink plenty of water. No soda. *(**BEVERLY** sighs.)* You've got to stay off your feet as much as possible. Please, Yonnie. I don't like what I'm seeing here. Your numbers are too high.

BEVERLY. "Doctors always say that shit. I'll be fine. Besides, what am I supposed to do? Stay off my feet? Please. This ain't no fairytale. Nobody is keeping me in a big castle so I can stay at home all day and put my manicured feet up. Even on my days off Mike don't come get the kids. Bed rest? I can't even get couch rest. My pops retired last year but he still picks up a few shifts doing greeting at Walmart. He comes when he can to play with the boys. Bless him. He's all I got."

TASHA. A few days before her due date she was admitted to the hospital. Her blood pressure was obscenely high.

BEVERLY. "Preeclampsia? What's that?"

TASHA. When the attending phoned me I rushed to the hospital to see about her. I was reviewing Yonnie's chart when the team came out of the O.R.

LAUREN. *(As other doctor.)* "I'm sorry. We did what we could."

    (Beat.)

TASHA. Yonnie had a baby girl. Her first. One of her aunts eventually named her, Grace. That day I finally met Yonnie's sons. Her eldest Joshua was holding an old Game Boy, her youngest boy John gripped a green race car.

LAUREN. *(As John.)* "Ma'am, are you the doctor?"

TASHA. That is only time I ever wanted to say no. *(To the child.)* Yes, dear. I'm one of the doctors here.

LAUREN. "Wow. I never met a Black doctor. Doctor, is Mommy OK? I'm an older brother now. Is the baby big? Is it a boy or a girl? Can I see them? Please? Can I see them?"

TASHA. I was devastated. Black mothers are dying every single day.

(**BEVERLY** *takes* **TASHA***'s hand.*)

LAUREN. That could have been me.

BEVERLY. She could have been me.

TASHA. It could have been—

(**LAUREN** *takes* **TASHA***'s hand.*)

ALL. Me.

(*The women embrace* **TASHA** *as she cries. The circle of sisterhood is tight.*)

Scene Twelve
Soccer Mom

TASHA. I'm gonna need something stronger than green tea to get me through this. What else we got?

LAUREN. Ask and she will provide.

(**LAUREN** *pulls a bottle of wine out of her purse.*)

BEVERLY. Nice!

TASHA. Wine? That's all you got? (**LAUREN** *flashes her a look.*) OK. OK. I'll take it.

(**LAUREN** *pours everyone a glass wine.*)

LAUREN. I think we all need a bit of something. You know I don't mess with anything stronger since you got me drunk freshman year. *(To the audience.)* Who else found out about that dark liquor in college? Show of hands!

TASHA. Guilty as charged. Hasn't stopped me from getting my drank on once in a while.

BEVERLY. Wait! You know each other from college?

TASHA. Yep.

LAUREN. Roommates. Learned a lot about each other in that dorm room.

TASHA. Close quarters makes for close friends or lasting enemies.

LAUREN. Or a little bit of both.

(**TASHA** *and* **LAUREN** *both laugh.*)

BEVERLY. I'm curious. What did becoming a mother teach you about yourself?

TASHA. *(As white parent at school.)* "Incredible! He really plays so well. He's simply a natural!"

BEVERLY *(As another white mother.)* "Please let him join the soccer team! All the kids head over to the field after school. Molly organizes the carpool and I'm sure she could run him over to the—"

LAUREN. *(To the other Mom.)* No. I don't want him on *that* soccer team. He actually belongs to a team on the east side. In the hood.

TASHA. "I see."

LAUREN. I'd seen enough. I had my fill after witnessing the Tyler twins scream at their mother to—

BEVERLY & TASHA. *(As bratty tween twins.)* "Shut! Up! Mom! Ughhhh!"

LAUREN. Nope! I didn't want my son to get any crazy ideas. Instead we trudge across town to the poorly maintained and poorly lit soccer fields in the mostly Black and Latinx neighborhood.

TASHA. *(As a Black soccer mom.)* "Hey! What's up?"

LAUREN. Good afternoon.

TASHA. "He on the team?"

LAUREN. Yes. I received an email from the organizers notifying me that today is the first practice.

TASHA. "They betta not have sent no email to my job. I'm not supposed to get non-work stuff. Damn."

BEVERLY. *(As another Black soccer mom.)* "You know I understand!"

TASHA. "Those socks are so cool."

LAUREN. Thanks! I let him pick them out himself. *(To audience.)* At the first practice I felt proud of my choice to diversify his life.

BEVERLY. "Girl, why is your son running like that?"

LAUREN. Oh no! I forgot to check to see if he needed new cleats!

TASHA. "What size does he wear?"

LAUREN. That pair is a five. So maybe a six?

TASHA. "Big feet for his age. *(To another Mom off stage.)* "Cynthia! Cynthia? Where did you get Shante's cleats this year? What? She's crazy. Oh yeah. You know that Walmart over off 183?"

LAUREN. Yes?

TASHA. "Cool. That's the one. Go to the Goodwill next to that Walmart. Girl, they have cleats in almost every size."

BEVERLY. Yep. That's the best Goodwill in town.

LAUREN. *(Surprised.)* Oh. OK. Yeah. Of course. I don't know why I didn't think of that. Yeah, the Goodwill next to the Walmart. *(Beat.)* I would never think of that. He was wearing $100 Nike's from Nordstrom.

BEVERLY. "Mommy, can Jamal come to my birthday sleepover?"

LAUREN. Jamal?

BEVERLY. "Yes. That tall kid at soccer. You know the one with the blonde 'fro hawk."

LAUREN. And the bad attitude? Jamal was a beast on the field. He even got taken out of a game for cursing out a ref! *(To son.)* Well. I don't know his Mom so...

BEVERLY. "Why don't you know her? I see you talking with her during the games sometimes."

LAUREN. Yes, but—

BEVERLY. "Why isn't she your friend, Mommy? You know all the kids at my school and their mothers *(Uttered loudly under his breath.)* and you don't even like them."

LAUREN. I'm sure that she doesn't want her child to stay overnight at a stranger's house.

BEVERLY. "Jamal already asked her and she said it's fine."

TASHA. *(As Jamal's mother.)* "Hey girl, thanks for inviting Jamal to the party. I'm on the night shift Saturday night. I can drop him off at?"

LAUREN. Six is great! They'll eat some pizza, play video games and watch a movie.

TASHA. "Cool! Girl, Jamal been dying to watch that zombie movie."

LAUREN. Actually I think they're planning to watch one of those Harry Potter films.

TASHA. "Um. Oh. Okay. So I'll pick him up around seven."

LAUREN. That's a little early in the morning.

TASHA. "What? No, seven in the evening! Girl, you know how it is. I need to sleep in and chill after my night shift. Those boys will be having fun anyway. We good?"

LAUREN. Well, I—

TASHA. "Cool! 'Preciate you!"

LAUREN. It was on. Not only would I need the will to survive a night with six ten-year-old boys but I'd have to get through babysitting bad ass Jamal the following afternoon once the other kids were picked up so they could head to tutoring or music lessons—

BEVERLY. "Miss?"

LAUREN. Yes, Jamal?

BEVERLY. "Your house is real nice."

LAUREN. Thank you.

BEVERLY. "It's really quiet here."

LAUREN. Usually.

BEVERLY. "You read all them books?"

LAUREN. Most of them, yes.

BEVERLY. "Whoa, I ain't never seen—"

LAUREN. You never saw?

BEVERLY. "Yeah, never seen these many books at somebody's house. If you read them already then why don't you give them to somebody else so they can read them too?"

LAUREN. That's a good question.

BEVERLY. "What are those fancy pieces of paper on your wall?"

LAUREN. Oh, that's my diploma from college. The other one is my diploma from graduate school.

BEVERLY. "Wow. I didn't know Black people went to those schools."

LAUREN. A few of us do.

BEVERLY. "Wow. That's dope. I'm gonna get me a couple of them."

LAUREN. I'm sure you will. *(Beat.)* You want to read that book? That's by James Baldwin.

BEVERLY. *(Reads slowly.)* "Notes of a Native Son."

LAUREN. When you're a bit older you should read *Manchild in a Promise Land*, *Invisible Man*, *Their Eyes are Watching* God, *The Bluest Eye*, and *The Color Purple*.

BEVERLY. "You got all of them?"

LAUREN. Yes, I do. You can borrow – no, you can have them when you're ready.

BEVERLY. "Cool. Thanks for having me over."

LAUREN. You're very welcome. Thank you for visiting our home.

TASHA. *(As son from off stage.)* "Jamal, come on! Show me how to do a header."

BEVERLY. "See you later."

LAUREN. I really hope so.

Scene Thirteen
Birds, Bees and Bombs

LAUREN. *(Notices that* **TASHA** *is clandestinely eyeing her cell phone.)* Tasha, I see what you're doing. We agreed that there will be no cell phones at the retreat.

TASHA. Don't worry about my business. Worry about yourself.

BEVERLY. Why don't I pull another question out of the basket?

LAUREN. *(Crosstalk between* **LAUREN** *and* **TASHA.***)* You don't have to be rude.

TASHA. I'm not being rude.

LAUREN. You just seem uptight.

TASHA. Uptight? Really? Do I?

LAUREN & BEVERLY. Yes!

TASHA. I'm just checking on something right quick.

LAUREN. Since today is about sharing—

TASHA. OK. OK. Prom night is coming and he said he's planning to ask someone. Today.

LAUREN. Is he seeing someone?

TASHA. Not that I've know about. I just hope whoever she is says yes. *(Phone pings!)* Wait! *(Reads text.)* He's got a date! He's got a date! His first date.

BEVERLY. Yay!

LAUREN. Wow! Who is it?

TASHA. *(Reading text.)* I'm dying to know.

> *(Shift to future.* **TASHA** *is speaking to her son.)*

BEVERLY. *(As son.)* "Be patient, Mom. I told you I want it to be a surprise.

TASHA. A surprise. OK. Well we need to rent you a tux, pick up some nice kicks, rent the limo, shop for a corsage—

BEVERLY. "I'll do that myself. On my own, Mom. I want everything to be perfect for—!"

TASHA. *(To audience.)* Who could it be? I'm just relieved that somebody wants to romance the only Black boy in the junior class. Who has he escorted into his adolescent fantasies? Is it a blonde? A wise Latina? A Filipina? Or maybe, just maybe it's a Black girl? *(Fingers crossed.)* I pray it's someone that looks like me. It doesn't matter because he finally has—

(The doorbell rings.)

BEVERLY. "A date!"

TASHA. I guess my baby is not a baby anymore.

(BEVERLY as the son answers the door.)

BEVERLY. "Hey! Wow. You look great. Come on in. *(He's holding his breath in anticipation.)* Mom, meet—

(Beat. TASHA is shocked. For a minute.)

Everett."

TASHA. *(TASHA takes it ALL in then she grows to realize that the past seventeen years just fell into place.)* Good evening, Everett. It's such a pleasure to meet you. Welcome to our home. *(Her son smiles.)*

Scene Fifteen
Moving Day

LAUREN. These kids grow up so fast.

TASHA. Can you imagine the day when your child finally leaves the nest?

> ([POMP AND CIRCUMSTANCE] *by Edward Elgar plays.*)

LAUREN. (*As college dean at welcome reception.*) "Welcome to Boutique Charming College, the small liberal arts institution with the big heart – and an even bigger endowment! (*Laughing at own joke.*) We're thrilled that you're joining our community of learners. As you can see from the map our four hundred plus acre campus allows for plenty of freedom."

BEVERLY. Freedom. I've been preparing for this day for nearly two decades.

LAUREN. "Parents, you should be very proud. Your children come to us today with brilliance and energy and after attending our quaint school for four years (or five years for those who like to get high) they'll be ready to remake the world!"

BEVERLY. As a Panther Mom (not to be confused with a Tiger Mom) I taught my Black child to climb every mountain in a world that wants to put shackles on my baby's body and imagination. I've got muscles you can't even see from lifting a ton of coal into the sun every day.

TASHA. And now you have a diamond that sparkles and shines.

LAUREN & TASHA. Your work is done.

> (*They all sit with the new strange stillness.*)

BEVERLY. The house is so quiet. Empty.

TASHA. And clean!

BEVERLY. Who will sit up with me watching movies? Who will I wait up for in the middle of the night?

LAUREN. You will still pray every night for their safety. He is young and Black and male. And living out in the world. Those nights are not fit for sleep.

BEVERLY. Is she really ready to be on her own at eighteen?

TASHA. You raised her. Look in the mirror and ask yourself.

BEVERLY. Will I ever be sure?

LAUREN. I just paid off my own loans and now need to borrow money to pay for his college tuition?

TASHA. I'm that little voice inside your head saying if you weren't so hell bent on being a single mom you'd have another income to draw on to pay for this Ivy league dream—

LAUREN. Yeah! I was so busy raising my son, I forgot to find a partner.

TASHA. But it's going to be alright. It's got to be alright.

(In dorm room.)

BEVERLY. Oh look, her roommate brought decorations for the room. What the hell? That's a Confederate flag!

TASHA. The changing same. The hope and the terror. The dance continues. *(She dances.)*

BEVERLY. Do you have all your classes?

LAUREN. *(As daughter.)* "Yes, Mom."

TASHA. *(Dancing.)* You know the steps.

BEVERLY. You have enough money for books?

LAUREN. "Yes, Mom."

TASHA. Two steps forward.

BEVERLY. Keep an eye on that roommate. In fact, here's the number to the local NAACP.

LAUREN. "Yes, Mom. Got it!"

TASHA. Two steps back.

BEVERLY. Should I buy you a school sweatshirt?

TASHA. Not a hoodie!

LAUREN. "I'm good."

TASHA. Slide.

BEVERLY. Text me or better yet call when you feel sad. Alone. Afraid.

LAUREN. "I'm good."

TASHA. Slide.

BEVERLY. Speak up for yourself if your professors say anything crazy.

LAUREN. "I'm good."

TASHA. Two steps forward.

BEVERLY. Respect your body. And everyone else's.

LAUREN. "Ugh! Mom! I'm good."

TASHA. Three steps back.

BEVERLY. Push yourself even when you think you have nothing left. Grit is sometimes more valuable than smarts.

LAUREN. "I'm good."

TASHA. Slide.

BEVERLY. What if something bad happens?

LAUREN. It's not.

BEVERLY. What if—

LAUREN. "Don't you trust me?"

BEVERLY. Yes, but I don't trust them.

TASHA. Cha Cha Cha.

LAUREN. "I stand here in this dorm room staring into your dark brown eyes and I'm telling you it's gonna be alright. I'm the person you raised. I'm good."

BEVERLY. I want to say, "But being good never saved anybody Black in this country." But instead I say – "I've got to hit the road now before it gets too dark."

LAUREN. I want to tell her – "I'm a little afraid to be without you but I'm also excited. I know there are some difficult things coming my way but there's gonna be amazing adventures too." Instead I say – "Be safe driving home. I love you, Mom."

BEVERLY. I want to say "I've never been prouder than I am right now. Or more afraid." Instead I say, "I love you too."

(They embrace powerfully.)

Coda
Next

LAUREN. Even though our kids will leave the nest one day—

TASHA. God willing and the creek don't rise!

LAUREN. —if we keep this up, we'll never be alone.

TASHA. You're stuck with me!

BEVERLY. For better or worse. For richer for poorer.

TASHA. Till death do us part!

LAUREN. You always gotta to take it there, Tasha!

>   *(They all laugh.)*

OK, ladies. The chef has prepared a yummy dinner for us this evening. Remember this is a planning dinner. *(To the audience.)* We need volunteers to organize the Mother's Day Brunch and a few more selections for our summer book club. Any other announcements?

>   (**TASHA** *raises her hand.* **LAUREN** *ignores her for a few beats.)*

Yes, Tasha.

TASHA. Thank you, Madame President! OK, I want to remind everyone that at next month's meeting there will be a shoe swap. Make sure you bring those shoes that are too tight for your bunions. Don't shake your head, I know you have more than a few pairs to contribute, Stacey!

LAUREN. Thank you, Tasha. Newcomers, we always end our meetings with a little tradition. Let's all join hands and recite the BBSM mantra. New members, please note that it is printed at the bottom of the retreat agenda. Got it? All together now.

ALL. We are proud Black single mothers and with our strong sisterhood behind us there's nothing we can't do.

> *(Upbeat music blares, consider an upbeat Black feminist anthem*.* **LAUREN, BEVERLY** *and* **TASHA** *hug, dance, and say goodbye to each other and to the audience members.)*

End of Play

---

* A license to produce THE MAMALOGUES does not include a performance license for any third-party or copyrighted music. Licensees should create an original composition or use music in the public domain. For further information, please see Music Use Note on page iii.